Lena Lenik

S.O.S.

Bernard Ashley

With illustrations by
Ollie Cuthbertson

Many thanks to the 27th Woolwich
(Wesley Hall) Scout Group

First published in 2017 in Great Britain by
Barrington Stoke Ltd
18 Walker Street, Edinburgh, EH3 7LP

www.barringtonstoke.co.uk

Text © 2017 Bernard Ashley
Illustrations © 2017 Ollie Cuthbertson

A CIP catalogue record for this book is available
from the British Library upon request

ISBN: 978-1-78112-571-7

Printed in China by Leo

Contents

Chapter 1
Down a Drain

"Are you all right?"

Lena Lenik nodded. "I'm good." She smiled at her friend – but it was a thin little effort.

Bobbie Kemp wasn't letting it go at that. "You came into the playground looking like your dinner-money's gone down a drain," she said.

"No, I'm all right."

"You can tell me, Leens," Bobbie said. "Best mates means best mates. What's up, girl?"

"I'm OK, Bobz. Believe me. Would I lie to you?"

"Yes!"

And Bobbie was right. Lena wasn't OK. A long way from it. That morning her mother had done something she'd never done before. She'd rung the school where she worked and said she was 'unwell'. And Lena could see that she was. Her face had lost its golden look and her swirly blonde hair looked more like a wet mop.

The sounds coming from the bathroom had been really scary.

"Mama, what is it?" Lena had called.

"Leave me! Go away, Lena!"

"You sound really bad."

"Don't come in! *Odejdź!*"

When Mama said things in Polish, she really meant them. Lena made Jan his breakfast and they walked together to school. He talked about football and Lena worried. Mama was never ill. She never missed a day teaching at Parkside. At the Polish Club she was always so lively, singing and dancing and chatting to everyone. But that wasn't the Mama in the bathroom today. She was sick, and it had to be something really, really bad.

"Lena Lenik, have you left your brain behind this morning? It seems like it to me."

Lena looked up as Ms Julien loomed over her.

"I didn't come to work to ask every question twice over!" the teacher went on. "Get that sleep out of your eyes." She made a snort down her nose like a runaway horse.

Callum Spike sneered across at Lena. But that didn't bother her today. She had something serious to worry about – her sick mother. That's what was turning her insides over.

Chapter 2
Tossing Pancakes

When Lena got home from school her dad was there. Tata was the Arts Officer at the London Polish Club. His working hours were set by the events he'd planned.

"How's Mama?" Lena could feel how her face was puffy with worry.

"She's fine." Tata nodded but he didn't smile.

Lena knew he was putting on a show. She always knew. Sometimes Tata played the piano at the Polish Club as if he was Chopin himself, but Lena could always see when he was jittery inside. His mouth went very small and he swallowed a lot. Right now he was wearing Mama's apron, tossing a pancake up out of the frying pan. And he didn't catch it as it came back down.

"Mama said she'll come from the bedroom when this cooking smell goes away," he said in his fast Polish way.

'But how can Mama be fine?' Lena thought. She was always the one to toss pancakes – she always caught them too, instead of making a mess on the floor.

"I'll go in and see her," Lena said.

"No thank you, Lena." Tata shook his head. "Mama will come when she's ready."

'Tata's not like Tata any more,' Lena thought. These days he was like Grandfather Stefan in Warsaw, as wooden as an old broomstick.

Things got worse. Mama came from the big bedroom with a smile on her face – but it didn't fool Lena. It was her polite smile.

"Lena. How was school today?" Mama's voice was croaky and faint.

"All right, Mama. How are you?"

"Oooh." Mama patted her stomach. "A funny tummy. And tired. You know ..." She lay down on the sofa. "Shut the door, Sunshine Girl. And the kitchen door. Food! I can't look at food." And she pulled a cushion over her face.

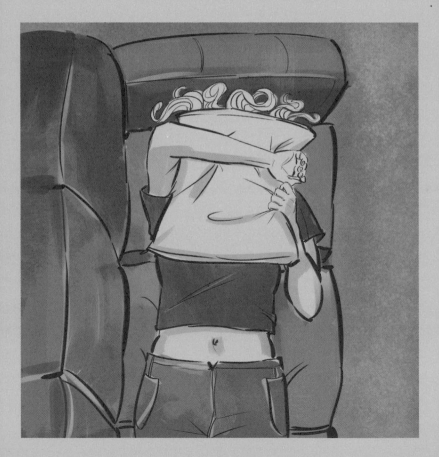

When Jan came bouncing in from Beavers Lena knew for sure that Mama was bad. He waved a badge and jumped about as if he'd won Olympic Gold.

"Mama! Tata! Look – I passed it today. My Collectors badge!" He held it out to Mama.

"*Brawo!*" She lifted the cushion from her face but she didn't raise herself up to look.

Tata made a big show of admiring the badge. "Congratulations!" he said, and he patted Jan on the head.

"Well done!" Lena joined in.

Jan was a Beaver and Lena was a Cub, and they both knew how important their award badges were. But Lena was way behind Bobbie, and now Jan was heading to be Chief Scout.

Jan held the badge against his arm. "Sew it on, Mama! Sew it on! Please!"

Mama stirred herself a little – but it seemed to take a real effort. "I'll do it before next week, Little Tiger," she said. "That cotton and those needles get real heavy sometimes."

Mama had tried to make a joke of it, but Lena could see she had lost her strength. She was fading away. Tata could see all this, too, couldn't he? Mama not fit to lift a needle? What did he think of that? But he just clapped his hands for supper.

Mama's face was under the cushion again. Poor Mama. Lena thought of how she had come from a village in Poland to this big city for a new and different life. Now look at her! Lena went cold. Was Mama's new life going wrong? Were things turning really bad?

Lena sat at the kitchen table and ate only a bite or two of Tata's pancakes. She had no appetite.

But Tata didn't seem to care. By the look of him, his mind was somewhere else as well.

Chapter 3
Nanna on a Bike

Lena had to tell Bobbie. They had been best mates ever since they started school. Almost like sisters, people said. Bobbie was funny, and she was ace at sharing secrets. Everything was better when it was shared with Bobz.

But, on Tuesday morning, Bobbie made everything worse. They were in the cloakroom, before class.

"Bobz," Lena began. "I've got to tell you about Mama ..."

"What about her?"

"She's not well ..."

"Aaah. I'm sorry, Leens ... I knew there was something. What's up with her?"

Lena told her – how ill Mama looked, the groans coming from the bathroom, Mama not eating, and not feeling up to lifting a needle.

"Oh my giddy aunt!" Bobbie looked horrified.

"What?" Lena went cold. "What, Bobz?"

"She sounds like Nanna Kemp," Bobbie said. "*Just* like Nanna Kemp."

Lena didn't like the sound of this.

"She had a dodgy stomach like your mum and kept being sick. Even a bit of bread turned her over. And she went all weak, so weak she said that she couldn't flick a flea off a fur coat."

Bobbie looked ready to cry. "And, Leens, you know what happened ..."

Lena did.

"... She died in North Park Hospital. From something bad inside of her. My mum won't talk about it even now."

Lena grabbed hold of Bobbie to steady herself. Poor Mama! At half term she'd splashed them all in the sea and built sandcastles with Jan. Just last week she'd danced a *mazurek* with the big doorman at the Polish Club. This had all happened so fast!

Ms Julien burst in like a Force 10 gale. "Classroom – now!" she shouted. "Cloakrooms are for hanging coats, not for hanging about!"

They did as they were told and went to their desks. But Lena wasn't really there at all. In her head she saw Nanna Kemp, dancing at one of Bobbie's parties. She had been funny and sparkly and young for her age. She wore T-shirts and jeans. She rode a bike with drop handlebars. She knew who Lady Gaga was. And she had got ill and died – from the same sorts of things Mama had got.

Lena's lovely Mama. Lena almost sobbed at the thought. What terrible bad luck had fallen down on her dear head?

Chapter 4
Spite and Hurt

When Lena got in from school, Mama was lying on the sofa trying to look like this was normal.

"You go to Cubs, Lena," she said. "Bobbie's mum will bring you home. Tata's got your things ready while I ..." But she stopped short, shut her mouth and closed her eyes.

Lena went into her bedroom. Her Cub uniform was laid out on the bed, but she didn't put it on. Instead, she came straight out again.

"I feel a little bit funny myself," she lied, and she held her stomach.

Mama seemed to be asleep and Tata was in a hurry and so he didn't hear her either.

Lena stayed at home. She felt bad about Bobbie, getting on with the Our World Challenge on her own. But Lena wasn't going to miss a second of being with Mama. These times were diamond.

*

Next day Lena told Bobbie why she hadn't gone to Cubs.

Bobbie put an arm around her. "Oh, poor Leens," she said.

But Callum Spike twisted his hateful face. He was nasty to Lena at every chance. "What's up with you, Lenik?" he sneered. "Your mum been sent back to Poland?"

Bobbie glared at him. "Her mum's ill, she won't eat nothing," she said. "You shut up and leave her alone, Spike."

But her words didn't soften the hate in his face.

"That won't hurt Lenik's mum," he snarled. "She's as fat as a pig."

Lena's eyes went thin. She wanted to cry – but she wouldn't. She wanted to punch his face – but she wouldn't do that, either. Tata and Mama were strong, and she was a Lenik, their flesh and blood, too. This boy was a toe-rag. And she would walk away from his hatred. That was what Mama and Tata would do whenever they needed to. And what was right for them was right for Lena, too.

Chapter 5
Crying like a Baby

Lena tried to be brave all day at school, but things seemed really bad when she got home. Mama was in the bedroom and Tata was wearing his tracksuit. So he wasn't going to work, and Lena knew he should be there tonight.

She went into the sitting room, and it looked different. The sofa had been pulled forward, nearer the two armchairs. What for? A family talk? Family talks were always serious. She heard Tata telling Jan to come out of his room right away. Nothing like this had ever happened before. Lena's insides turned over. What were Tata and Mama going to say? What terrible news was coming?

She and Jan sat silent on the sofa and Tata went to the bedroom to fetch Mama – who walked in with a little smile on her face. But Lena didn't buy that for a moment. Her mother was just being very brave.

Lena shut her eyes and bit her lips. She was not going to cry. Whatever this news might be, she was not going to make it worse by crying like a baby.

They all sat and looked at each other.

Tata gave a funny little cough. "We have something to tell you both," he said.

Lena's insides seemed to drain away. She tried to hold Jan's hand, but he pushed her off.

Tata looked at Mama. He nodded to her. She was going to tell them the bad news herself.

Mama sat up as stiff as a queen – then all of a sudden her face split with the biggest, brightest smile in the world.

"I'm going to have a baby!" Mama said. "*We're* going to have a baby!" She punched the air and whooped like a winner.

"A new brother or sister!" Tata was beaming. "A new little Lenik!"

And now Lena cried. She had not cried for Callum Spike, and she had not cried in front of Mama. But now she cried for the Lenik family and its happiness, and her crying was loud and long and very wet.

She wiped her face and went to Mama for a hug. She went to Tata for a kiss. And she turned to Jan for – what?

"Let's give them a Wolf," Jan said. It was a special thing that Lena's Cubs did to say 'well done'.

Lena and Jan stood side by side.

"One!" they shouted, and they punched the air with their fists.

"Two!" they shouted and punched the air again.

Then, "Three!" – and – "Wolf!"

They yelled it at the tops of their voices and pointed straight at Mama and Tata.

Mama and Tata knew what came next. They stood up. *"Raz, dwa, trzy – Wilf!"* they shouted back, punching then pointing at the two of them.

"A new Polish Cub in the pack," Tata said. "*Brawo!*"

They all sat down and Mama told them that the baby was why she'd been feeling bad. She'd had morning sickness, like lots of other pregnant women. But hers was evening sickness too.

"I never had it before," Mama said.

"What a relief!" Lena blew out her cheeks. "But why didn't you tell us?"

"We wanted to be sure, Sunshine Girl. But we've been to the clinic today, and everything is fine."

Lena felt so light she could have floated up to the sky. All the worry had been lifted from her. What a day to remember!

Then Tata took Jan to the park for a kick-about, and Lena went out onto the balcony with

Mama. They sat together as the sun sank low over the city.

"At school we've learned about babies," Lena said. "My class had 'Living and Growing' lessons. We saw all about making and having a baby – with a film of a real baby being born. I can tell you all about it. From the start to the finish – with the baby coming out and everything. Just ask me. Any time."

"Thank you." Mama gave her a kiss on the forehead. "I will if I need to, but I do know a bit about it myself." She patted her stomach. "From my end of things." And she laughed like the old Mama – loud enough to make people stare up from the car park.

Lena wasn't quite sure what was so funny but she laughed too. She looked across at the sun dipping down behind the trees.

Mama was looking, too. "Round and round we go," she said. "The earth on its spin. A day dies, and then another is born. The cycle of life."

Lena nodded. That was true. But right now she was just so happy to be thinking about the getting born part of the cycle, and not the part that had scared her.

Chapter 6
Another Surprise

Mama's morning and evening sickness soon came to an end, and Lena started joining in with the special exercises Mama did to get ready for the birth of the baby. They did deep breathing, and fast panting like a dog. They lay on the floor and did yoga things with their hips. And Lena was thrilled to see the black and white photo from Mama's scan.

"Look, Mama – there's the little legs, and the arms, and the hands!" she said. "And the feet, the fingers and, ah, look! The tiddly toes!" Lena put her ear to Mama's belly.

"What can you hear, Sunshine Girl?" Mama asked.

There was a swishing and gurgling sound. Lena looked up at her mother, deadly serious. "My baby sister says she can't wait to get out of there and come to Cubs with me."

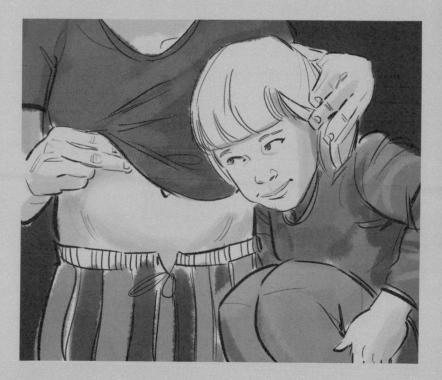

Mama wagged her finger. "Sister? Even Tata and I don't know if the baby's a boy or a girl. We just want a nice surprise."

*

But another surprise came first. One evening soon after, Mama and Tata took Lena and Jan into the kitchen.

Lena frowned at Jan and then turned to her parents. "What's this about?" she asked.

"We've been to the baby clinic today," Mama said. She pulled a little card from her pocket. She fixed it on the fridge door. "There!"

Lena and Jan looked at it.

North Park Hospital Home Birth Service Midwife number – 020 8539 6278

Lena frowned. "*Home Birth Service?*"

Tata nodded. "That's right. Mama's going to have the baby here at home."

Mama's eyes were big and happy. "The midwife says everything's good for a home birth. I've had two babies with no problems ..."

"And we were perfect!" Lena shouted. "Can we be here when the baby is born?"

"Of course," Tata said. "Unless you're at school. Just keep yourselves out of the way, that's all."

Jan pulled a face at that, until Tata promised to buy him a new computer game for the big day. "And, Lena, you can choose something, too," Tata said.

But later, when Lena went to bed, she didn't think about any of that. She thought how great the home birth would be. She would hear the baby's first cry almost as soon as Mama did.

And the baby would see *her* before almost anyone else in the world. Wow!

Those thoughts kept Lena awake for a long time – hearing the sound of that first cry in her head, and seeing the new baby's face.

Chapter 7
The Birthing Kit

After Cubs one evening Lena told Bobbie what would happen.

"When Mama thinks the baby's coming she's got to phone the midwife service," she said. "Then they come to the flat for the birth. We've already got all the stuff that's needed. It's called the birthing kit."

"That makes sense," Bobbie said.

"When the baby's born I can be third person to hold her," Lena told her. "After the midwife's checked everything's all right."

"Don't drop it, Leens," Bobbie said. "Babies don't bounce, you know. But you won't be in with your mum at the – you know – actual time, will you?"

"No, we'll be in our own rooms and we'll have our special presents. Jan's got a computer game and I've got an amber necklace."

"You can't play with that, girl."

"No, but I can admire myself in the mirror!" Lena preened and they both laughed. "But I'd swap my necklace for one of your badges any day." Lena was looking at Bobbie's Cub uniform.

"Never mind that," Bobbie said. "You just get plenty of kip from now on. You're gonna need it, Leens. Babies don't half yell."

"It'll sound like music to me," Lena told her. "No problem, Bobz."

*

But there was a problem – and it wasn't about Lena's sleep. It came on the first of June, which was a big night at Cubs. Bobbie had passed her final Challenge so she was getting the Chief Scout's Silver Award – the top award given to a Cub.

Bobbie's mum and dad were there, and so was the Head Scout of the district. The *Wolf!* shout for Bobbie was so loud it made the lights swing. Lena was one of the loudest – but still she couldn't stop a twist of envy pinging inside her. Imagine getting a badge like that! Perhaps she would, one day – but this was Bobbie's night, and Lena gave her a proper big hug when they said goodbye.

"Well done, Bobz," she said. "Cubs for ever!"

But Lena soon forgot about Cubs. First of all, the lift in their block wasn't working and she had to walk up to the 5th floor. And when she got there Jan was jumping up and down on the landing as if the floor was red hot.

"Lena!" he called. "Quick! It's Mama!"

He pulled her into the flat, where Mama was calling from her bedroom.

"That you, Lena? In here, girl! Get to the kitchen and phone the midwife! My mobile's gone dead. Say the baby's coming."

The baby's coming?

"But, Mama – it's not due till next week."

"This baby doesn't care about next week!" Mama said. "Ask for Midwife Rose. Tell her, 'Dagmara Lenik at Eagle Rise has started.' You got that? *Started*."

"Got it."

Lena ran to the phone. Her skin felt frozen. The baby was coming – a week early. Oh, help! Tata wasn't here – and Mama was growling like a bear in the bedroom. This was all happening for real!

With careful fingers Lena tapped in the midwife's number.

But the phone just rang and rang.

'Hurry, midwives, hurry, hurry! *Szybko!*' Lena thought. 'Be quick and answer the phone! *This is an S.O.S. call!*'

Chapter 8
Grid-Lock

"North Park Midwife Service," a soft voice said. "Rose Barnett speaking."

At last!

Lena took a deep breath. "My mother says, 'Dagmara Lenik at Eagle Rise has *started*,'" she said.

But Midwife Rose sounded worried. "Have you seen the news, Lena?" she said. "There was a bad accident on the A104. All the roads are grid-locked."

Help!

"Just keep your mum calm and comfortable," the midwife said.

"Yes."

"I'll be there as quick as I can," Rose went on. "Who else is with you?"

"My little brother."

"Oh. I see. But you'll be all right. It could be hours yet. And your mother's one of my stars. She's got her head stuck on the right way."

But right now it sounded as if Mama's head was coming off altogether. She was shouting out in Polish, which meant the pain was bad.

"*Co zaból! Co zaból!*"

Lena ran for the bedroom.

"Lena, this child won't wait!" Mama cried.

Jan was still jumping.

"Phone Tata!" Lena told him. "On his mobile."

"Lena!" Mama yelled. "This baby's coming!"

Mama was perched on the bed, her face wet with sweat and her legs pulled up. But as the pain passed she calmed again. "I felt something this morning but I thought it was baby kicking extra hard ..." she said.

Lena told her what Midwife Rose had said about the traffic. She looked at her watch. "I'll time the pains, OK, Mama?"

Jan put his head round the bedroom door. "Tata's coming. He's running to the Underground."

"Be quick, my Borys! *Szybko!* Be quick!" Mama groaned.

It was not even two minutes until the next pain came – and by then the air was filled with half the words in the Polish dictionary.

Mama couldn't keep still. "Where's that midwife?" she cried. "We need her here right now. I can't stop this baby. Get Mrs

Sparrow, Lena. It's emergency, Sunshine Girl, emergency!"

Lena ran to next-door's flat. But Mrs Sparrow didn't answer, not the knocker and not the bell. And Old Mr Bolt across the landing wouldn't be any use. She ran back to Jan.

"Stay on the landing and grab Mrs Sparrow the second she comes," she said.

"Lena," Mama cried. "Bring that birthing kit. Ooooh! Aaaah! *Heeeeelp!*" Mama's head was in the air, her mouth was wide open, and Lena knew she was panting hard to stop herself from pushing. "Where … are … they?" Mama was shouting louder than Ms Julien in the playground. "Where … is … anybody?"

*

Tata was at Victoria Underground station, pushing onto a crowded train. He forced himself

on and the doors closed – and then opened
again.

  "*Please keep all bags away from the doors.*"

  Tata swallowed hard. "Hold on, my
Dagmara!" he said. "Hold on!"

The doors closed at last and the train pulled out. But it was a long way from Victoria to Wood Street – two changes and then an overground train. Would he ever make it in time?

*

Midwife Rose was in her nippy little car – in a long line waiting to get onto North Park Road. And North Park Road itself was another long line, waiting to get onto Greenford Road.

She picked up her mobile. Mrs Lenik had started – but this stage sometimes took hours. Even if it didn't, midwives were used to giving help down the phone.

Just then the traffic moved a metre and the car behind hooted. Rose moved on, too, but she dropped the phone and it slid under her seat.

"I'm coming!" she shouted to no one and everyone.

But she wasn't coming yet. The gap had been a lorry turning around to go back the way it had come, that was all. Rose was stuck again – and however much she scrabbled under the seat she couldn't find her mobile.

She looked in the rear-view mirror and saw what a helpless look she'd got on her face.

"Hold on, Dagmara!" she called.

Chapter 9
Lena Does Her Best

Mama couldn't hold on.

"I've got to push!" she shouted at Lena. "*Oooooh!* It's coming, girl, it's coming. I've got to push! Go wash your hands – run."

Lena had already laid a patchwork of big bath towels on the bedroom floor. She had put the birthing kit close by, and set a bowl of warm water ready.

She ran back from the bathroom and helped Mama to get off the bed.

"Unless that Rose comes soon it's you and me, Sunshine Girl!" Mama said as she sat down on the towels with her back against the bedroom wall. "I'm the mother and you're the midwife!"

Lena kneeled next to her. Mama had her knees wide apart, her fists clenched and her head back. Lena thought of the baby she'd seen in the school film – its little head coming out, then the rest of its body. The thought made her

shiver – but not with cold, and not with fear. It was with the shivery thrill of being tested.

"Cubs, do your best!"

Well, Lena would. She would if she had to.

*

Tata had to change trains at the next station. But what was that on the display board?

Delays on the Victoria Line.
Next train – 10 minutes.

He still had a long way to go. Too far. But a taxi would take a lot longer. He just had to stand on the platform and wait, and wait.

*

Midwife Rose also had to wait, and wait. A little move forward gave her some hope – but it went next to nowhere. She was starting to feel hot with worry. Mrs Lenik was not the sort to panic, but all the same.

"Please take your time, little baby," she said to herself. "Take your time, for goodness' sake."

*

But the baby didn't take its time. Mama was in a sweat, panting on all fours on the floor.

"Ooooh! Aaaaah! I ... can't ... hold off! It's coming! It's coming – any second! Ooooh! Borys! Borys! Ooooh! Aaaah! *Oh, Leeeeeenah!*"

Lena helped Mama lean against her, ready for the baby to come out. She folded another soft towel and laid it close by on the floor. Soon there was blood on the towel, but Lena knew this would happen and it was all right.

"What can you see? Aaaaaah! Can you see a head? Ooooooh!" Mama was pushing hard from inside herself, shouting in Polish and English. "*Pomocy!* Help me! *Pomocy!*"

Lena was brave and looked. And, yes, she could see something that hadn't been there a moment ago. It had to be the top of a head.

"I can see it!" she cried. "I can see it!"

"Aaaaah!" Mama's face was scarlet all over from her straining. "Come on, you baby! Ooooh! Help me, little child, be quick!"

Her voice was not how Lena had ever heard it – high and loud and young.

Lena held Mama's shaking body. Then, yes! The head was coming out, more and more as Mama pushed – a real little head coming into the world, here in their flat. It was the most wonderful thing Lena had ever seen. Her eyes filled with tears as she put her hands ready to hold this special baby.

"Aaaaaaah! Leeeenah! *Aaaaaaah!*"

It sounded like Mama's voice was coming
from a different world. But with a last big push
the baby came all the way out. First its head
with a little wrinkled face. Next the shoulders
and the tiny arms. Then the skinny wet body.
And last, two strong little legs that started
kicking the moment they were in the air. It was

real, alive, and it slipped into Lena's arms like a tender gift.

"Yes!" she shouted. "I've got it!"

The baby gave a cry and a hiccup and a yell. "Yaaaa! Yaaaa!" – its first cry was so loud that Lena couldn't believe it. She'd been right – it was the most musical sound she'd ever heard.

And now Mama was sitting up to see her baby. She was breathing hard, her eyes were wide, and tears of joy were rolling down her bright cheeks.

"It's our baby!" She looked up at the picture of St Nicholas above the bed. "Thank you, thank you, thank you, thank you!"

Lena was crying, too. "And ... I tell you something, Mama. It's a girl. It's a lovely ... baby girl!"

"Yes, child. Yes!"

And then there came the sudden slam of the door and in ran Tata, with almost no breath left in him. "Sweet heavens! Sweet heavens!" he cried.

"She's a girl!" Lena told him. "We've had a girl!"

Tata hugged and kissed Mama, helped her onto the bed and pulled a cover around her, Lena close by all the time. He reached out his arms to her as she cradled the baby – but he didn't hold her. He pulled a towel from the birthing kit and put it round the baby's small body to keep it warm in Lena's arms.

"You keep holding her," he said. "I'll do the rest."

He was going to cut the cord that joined the baby to Mama. But Lena could see that his mouth had gone small and he was swallowing hard.

And he didn't have to do it. At that moment Midwife Rose came in with Jan, puffing and panting as if she was the one who'd given birth.

"That traffic! ... Those stairs! ... This baby!"

She unzipped her bag, pulled out her apron and gloves and put them on. She lifted the baby from Lena's arms and with no fuss at all she cut the cord, held her up for Dagmara to kiss, then carried the baby to the bathroom.

Tata gave Lena and Jan the biggest cuddles in the world. "My children, we say thank you to God and hello to our new little London baby."

Rose came from the bathroom and gave Mama the baby. "Here she is, Dagmara, with everything all right. Ten fingers and ten toes and lungs for blowing up balloons."

"That's a blessing." Mama cradled her new daughter, who began to settle down. "I was born like this in Sarnowo village," she said, and she kissed the baby on the head. "The snows were high in the village and no one could get to us. My big sister Aneta helped give birth to me." She looked up at Lena. "Your aunty Aneta was my Sarnowo midwife – and now you've been a real Sarnowo midwife to me." And in her joy Mama held out a hand to Lena and cried and cried and cried.

"Well, I don't know about Sarnowo," Rose said. "But your Lena's a London midwife all right." Smiling at Lena, she folded her apron and carefully took off her NHS Midwife badge.

What was she doing?

Rose pinned the special badge onto Lena's Cub uniform, at just the spot where the Chief Scout's Silver Award should go. It was like the Queen presenting a medal.

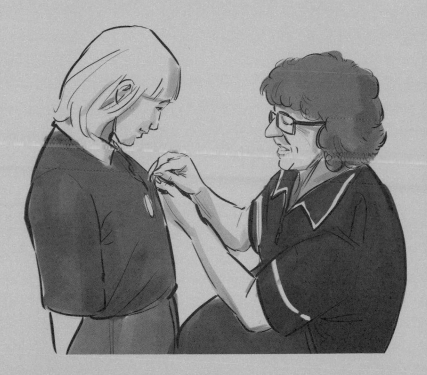

"Thank you," Lena said. "Thank you."

Lena stood up tall. She had been given a better badge than any other badge in the world. She patted it and looked around the room. They were all looking at her, even the baby, who seemed to have her big blue eyes fixed on Lena.

Lena felt so proud. She couldn't wait to tell Bobbie. She would wear this badge everywhere and she would keep it for ever – unless she had reason to give it to her own child one day.

And that would be a day to remember, too, wouldn't it?